Beep Beep THE ROAD RUNNER

Tumbleweed Trouble

story by Jack Woolgar

illustrated by Leon Jason Studio

A GOLDEN BOOK • NEW YORK

Western Publishing Company, Inc.
Racine, Wisconsin 53404

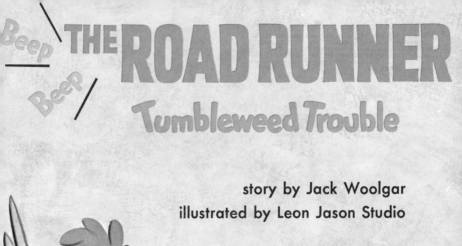

"Beep! Beep!"

The familiar sound brought Wile E. Coyote rushing out of his cave. He saw the Road Runner family — Poppa and Momma Beep and the three little Beeps — streaking across the desert at terrific speed.

"Where are those crazy birds going now?" Wile E. wondered out loud.

He jumped into his car and followed them to the old deserted railroad depot. He hid behind a big rock.

The Beep family lined up on the road in back of the depot.

Suddenly Wile E. heard a loud *TOOT TOOT!* The five Beeps smiled and stretched out their long necks.

TOOT TOOT! A fast express thundered by. The Road Runners took off after it!

Wile E. grinned. "Wow — this I've got to see!"

He was driving as fast as he could when he caught up with the train. But the Road Runners were going faster. They were way ahead!

Wile E. didn't see any passengers
on the train. But the engineer was
shaking his fist at the Road Runners.

The train stopped at the new depot. Wile E. hopped out and saw the Beep family strutting proudly up and down.

He walked over to the engine cab and grinned at the engineer. "So you can't beat the Road Runners either!"

The big redheaded engineer growled, "I've got to, or lose my job. Today was the test run of this new, speedy train. But tomorrow I'll carry passengers and my boss. If they see the Road Runners beat me, I'm sunk."

"Why?" asked Wile E.

"Because this is supposed to be the fastest train in the West. If it can't beat a bunch of beeping birds, nobody will believe it!"

Wile E. scratched his head. "Don't worry, mister. I'll think of something to slow them down."

On the way home, Wile E. stopped at Bugs Bunny's filling station. "Look, Bugs," he said. "I need your help. The Beeps are going to race that new fast train tomorrow morning. If they win, the engineer might lose his job. Let's block the road with tumbleweeds."

"How will that stop the Road Runners?" Bugs asked. "They'll just run around them."

"Maybe." Wile E. grinned. "But it will slow them down. And that's all that matters."

That afternoon, Bugs, Wile E., and some friends hauled truckloads of big tumbleweeds from all over the desert. Soon the road between the depots was covered with them.

Early the next morning, Wile E. and
Bugs drove to the old depot. They hid
behind the rock and waited for the
Road Runners.

"Beep! Beep!" The Road Runners were on time. They chattered excitedly when they saw the rows of big tumbleweeds. Wile E. grinned.

TOOT TOOT! The express roared past. It was crowded with passengers.

"Beep! Beep!" The Road Runners sprang into action. Poppa Beep hopped onto a tumbleweed. He kept his balance like an expert logroller. Momma Beep and the little Beeps followed.

Passengers waved as the five Beeps kept the tumbleweeds rolling. Like acrobats, they jumped from one tumbleweed to the next. Before long, they were ahead of the train.

"Let's go, Bugs!" Wile E. shouted. "We've got to stop them!"

They jumped in the car and started to follow. But the Beeps were rolling all the tumbleweeds right in front of them. There were so many that they couldn't even see the road.

When Wile E. and Bugs finally arrived at the depot, they saw a crowd gathered around the Road Runners. The engineer's boss was talking to them and smiling.

"Thanks for the thrill you gave our passengers," he said. "They liked the race so much, we're going to make it a daily feature. I'll see that you all get medals for your help."

"What about me?" Wile E. asked. "The tumbleweeds were my idea!"

A big man in a sheriff's uniform tapped Wile E.'s shoulder. "So you're the one who littered the road with tumbleweeds, huh? You've got until noon to clean up the mess, or you'll go to jail!"

Wile E. looked around for Bugs, but the smart bunny was gone. He moaned and began clearing the tumbleweeds off the road by himself.

It didn't make the poor coyote feel better when he heard Poppa Beep say to his family: "Blazing speed is what we've got. It put poor Wile E. on the spot!"

"Beep! Beep!" The gleeful Road Runners raced away to play in the desert.